EMMA

IS ON THE AIR

BIG NEWS!

EMMA

IS ON THE AIR

#1: BIG NEWS!

by IDA SIEGAL

illustrations by
KARLA PEÑA

SCHOLASTIC INC.

Text copyright © 2015 by Ida Siegal
Illustrations copyright © 2015 by Scholastic Inc.

This book is being published simultaneously in hardcover by Scholastic Press.

All rights reserved. Published by Scholastic Inc. SCHOLASTIC, SCHOLASTIC PRESS, and associated logos are trademarks and/or registered trademarks of Scholastic Inc.

No part of this publication may be reproduced, stored in a retrieval system, or transmitted in any form or by any means, electronic, mechanical, photocopying, recording, or otherwise, without written permission of the publisher. For information regarding permission, write to Scholastic Inc., Attention: Permissions Department, 557 Broadway, New York, NY 10012.

This book is a work of fiction. Names, characters, places, and incidents are either the product of the author's imagination or are used fictitiously, and any resemblance to actual persons, living or dead, business establishments, events, or locales is entirely coincidental.

ISBN 978-0-545-68692-1

10 9 8 7 6 5   16 17 18 19 20/0

Printed in the U.S.A.   40

First printing 2015

Book design by Sharismar Rodriguez

FOR MY CHILDREN, EVAN AND CELIA.
YOU ARE MY FOUNTAIN OF HUMOR AND JOY.
THANK YOU FOR GIVING ME EMMA.

CONTENTS

CHAPTER ONE

Famous

IF you have to do a chore, you might as well set the table. That's my chore. It's better than cleaning your room, or scrubbing the toilet, or worse . . . changing your baby sister's diaper trash can! Yuck. Plus, when you set the table, you can practice being famous.

"Plaaaate! Everybody needs a plaaaate!" I sang as I skipped around our faded wooden table Sunday evening. That's how *famous* people

set the table. They sing and set at the same time. Singing is a very famous job.

"Fooork! Now everybody needs a fooork!"

My cat, Luna, joined in to help me. She likes to be famous, too. *"Meeeoow! Meow, meow, meeeoow,"* she sang along.

Luna has the softest brown fur you've ever seen. It makes me think of chocolate pudding. My hair is the same brown as Luna's, except with curls and really long. Like chocolate pudding Slinkies. If I stretch my pudding Slinkies out, I can practically sit on them. I'm eight years old—and so are my curls. I've never cut my hair before. Next year, my curls will turn nine!

I whipped my eight-year-old pudding-Slinky curls from one side to the other, famous-style. Then I used a spoon for a microphone and sang as loud as I could, *"Spoooon, glorious spoooon! Next to the knife youuu go!"*

Down the hall, my baby sister started crying.

"Emma! What are you doing out there?" called my mom from the kitchen.

"I'm setting the table, Mom, like you told me to," I called back.

"I don't think I told you to wake up your sister," she said, walking into the dining room. "Though I suppose she had to get up for dinner soon, anyway."

Mom went to get Mia, and I continued setting the table.

"Knife and napkin. Knife and napkin. Cut and wipe and make it happen!" I sang in my extra-famous voice.

Then Papi yelled from the living room.

"*¿Qué pasa aquí?*" he asked.

That's Spanish. It means, "What's going on here?"

"*¡Nada!*" I yelled back. That means, "Nothing!"

My papi is from a whole other country called the Dominican Republic. They speak Spanish there. That's why I call him Papi—it's like saying "Daddy," but in Spanish. You say it like this: "PAH-pee."

"Dinner's almost ready. Isn't that right, Mia?" Mom said as she put baby Mia in her green high chair next to the table. My mom is not from the Dominican Republic. She's from here—New York City. That's where we live. Our neighborhood is called Washington Heights. It's at the very tippy-top of Manhattan.

"GAGA BABA BOO," Mia said in baby language.

Mom answered her in grown-up baby language. "Yes, I know you're ready for dinner! Oh, you're so cute . . . coo, coo, coo . . . look at that smile."

Mia is pretty cute. But baby talk is for babies, and I'm eight, so I ignored them and kept singing and setting the table.

"Seriously, Emma," said my dad. "I'm trying to watch the news; please pipe down a bit."

The living room is right next to the dining room, so when Papi started watching the news on our TV, I could see it, too.

Ugh. The news. It's just so boring. It's horribly, ridiculously, terrifyingly boring!

"But, Papi, I haaaate the news!" I groaned. "It's sooo boring."

"Watching the news while you set the table won't kill you," Mom said.

On the TV, there was a man and a woman sitting at a big news desk. It was blue and yellow and looked like it glowed in the dark. They started talking about a boring man with a boring tie. And then they talked about a boring doctor, and he talked about a boring doctor thing.

Then I could feel it. I could feel the boredom kicking in. It tingled as it entered through my ears and eyes . . . and then the boredom started oozing through my whole body and I couldn't make it stop! I really was going to be bored to death! I was about to tell my papi to call an ambulance when . . . I saw her.

Suddenly there was a woman on the TV. A fancy-looking newswoman. She was standing on the street, and there were lots of police cars behind her. She had shiny brown hair, a fabulous red coat, and glossy pink lips. Her cheeks were rosy with blush, and her eyelashes were long and black. She was wearing a big white pearl necklace, and she was holding a microphone with a colorful cube on top. She was amazing.

"Police say the robber smashed the glass window," she was explaining. "He grabbed ten gold watches and ran away down the street."

She was not boring at all. She looked so . . . she just looked so . . . so *special*.

I placed the last cup on the table and raced over to the sofa where Papi was sitting.

"Papi, who was that?" I asked hurriedly.

"Oh, her? She's a reporter. I forget her name," he replied.

"A news reporter? Do you think she's famous?"

"Well, I suppose," Papi said.

"Aha! I knew it! I knew she was famous. I'm going to be just like her!" I declared.

"But, Emma, wait . . . that's not why she—"

But I had already run out of the room. A news reporter. I knew right away this was how I was going to be famous! Besides, how hard could it be?

CHAPTER
TWO

News-Reporter Famous

THE next morning, I skipped downstairs to the kitchen table and landed in my chair with a thud and a smile.

"You're in a good mood, Emma," Mom said, smiling back at me. She spooned some cereal into baby Mia's open mouth. Papi was reading the newspaper.

"I sure am, Mom," I said. It was true. I was in a great mood! "Wanna know why?"

"Spill it," Mom replied.

"Because famous people are always in a good mood. And now I'm going to be famous! A famous news reporter!"

"Aha," Mom said. "That sounds exciting! Although I'm not sure famous people are *always* happy . . ."

"Oh, yes, they are," I corrected.

"Even so, Emma, not all news reporters are famous," Papi chimed in. "For example, I'm a newspaper reporter. I write very important stories for the *New York Herald*, and I'm not on TV," he explained.

"Papi, I know. But newspaper reporters aren't the cool kind. Sorry, but they're not."

"Oh, so TV news reporters are the cool kind?" Papi asked.

"Yup!" I told him.

Papi gave me a look and then made a *humph* sound. Then he went back to reading his newspaper.

"So, Mom," I continued, "I'm going to be a famous *TV* news reporter. How do I do that?"

"Why don't you ask your uncool father? He probably knows," she said with a smile.

I turned back to Papi. He wasn't smiling. "I'm

sorry I called you uncool," I said. "Maybe that wasn't very nice."

"That's okay," Papi replied.

"So can you show me how to be a TV news reporter?

A famous one? *¿Por favor?*" That means "please" in Spanish. Papi likes it when I speak Spanish.

"Okay, okay, *mija*. Only because you're so smart and cute and I love you!" Then he leaned over to kiss my forehead.

My papi is the best!

"What do I need to do?" I asked.

"Well, you need to find a news story," explained Papi.

"But how do I do that?"

"You have to pay attention to what's going on around you. And when you see something happen that you think people need to know about, you write a story about it."

"Like we did in school, when I wrote about the adventures of Luna? How Luna went shopping at the supermarket to buy cat food, but then she couldn't find the cat food, so she started climbing the shelves. Remember when I wrote that?"

"Yes," said Papi. "That was an excellent story. But let me ask you something: Was that a true story? Did it really happen?"

"No!" I giggled. "Papi, cats can't go grocery shopping. I made it up."

"Aha! That's the difference," Papi said in an excited voice. "A news story isn't something you can just make up. It has to be something that actually happened. It has to be *true*. Your job is to tell everyone about things that happened. Things that are true."

Oh, I thought. "Now I get it, Papi." He smiled. "Like, I could tell a news story about how you were making macaroni and cheese the other night." I started giggling as I remembered. "But you forgot to take the cheese packet out of the box before you poured the macaroni into the pot of boiling water. So the cheese packet fell into the boiling water!"

Papi and I both cracked up.

"Okay, yes," he said, "technically, that would be a story about something that's true, something that did really happen." Papi sighed like he was embarrassed. "But is that something people really need to know about?"

"If they want a good laugh, it's something they'd *want* to know about." I giggled some more.

"Okay, *que gracioso*. Very funny. But, Emma, a news story should be something people *need* to know. When you go to school today, think about things like that."

"Okay, Papi," I agreed. But I still wasn't sure what kinds of things people needed to know about.

"Come on, Emma ... it's time," Mom called from the hall. "School bus will be downstairs in five minutes."

I grabbed my backpack and my coat, and Mom and I headed out the door.

CHAPTER THREE

Wormburger

MORNING, Emma, take a seat," said Bus Driver Dan. I waved good-bye to Mom on the sidewalk and started climbing onto the bus. I could see Bus Driver Dan's sweaty armpits. Eww. Maybe I should do a news story about sweaty armpits! Ha-ha. That'd be . . . well . . . gross.

Just keep paying attention, Emma. What do people need to know about?

I walked down the aisle of the school bus and sat down next to my best friend, Sophia.

"Hi, Emma," she said with a big smile.

"Hi, Sophia!" I said back.

Sophia and I are perfect-match friends. We are opposites in just the right ways. She likes to talk a little bit, and I like to talk A LOT. We always have great conversations. Sophia likes to dance, and I like to sing. We make our own

music videos. But most importantly, Sophia's favorite color is light lavender with sparkles, and my favorite color is bright purple with shimmers! We always go great together.

"Guess what, Sophia?" I shouted.

"What?" she asked.

"I'm going to be famous!"

"I know. You've told me that like a hundred times before," said Sophia.

"No, this time I'm really going to be famous," I explained. "I'm going to be a famous news reporter! Just like on TV."

"A news reporter? You're going to be on TV?"

"Yup, yup!"

"Wow. That's awesome."

A few minutes later, the bus pulled up in front of our school.

Sophia and I got off the bus and went to class together. We have the same third grade teacher, Miss Thompson. She is the best!

That morning in class, we did decimals in math. No news story there. We created a collage to make a rain forest. It was a fun project, but a boring news story. Then we had to write a poem about the animals in the rain forest. Ugh. Definitely not a good idea for a news story. I hate writing. It's too hard. The day was half over, and I still hadn't found a good story for my news report.

"Time for lunch, everybody!" called Miss Thompson. We lined up and walked to the cafeteria. Sophia and I sat next to each other at our usual table near the window.

"Hi, Emma," said Shakira. She and Lizzie sat down with us.

"Hi, Shakira. Hi, Lizzie!" I said.

Shakira and Lizzie are also perfect-match friends. Shakira knows everything about purses, bracelets, and hair bands. Lizzie knows everything about tights, necklaces, and hats. They are always accessorized. Shakira loves to play soccer. Lizzie loves to watch tennis. They talk about sports a lot. But most importantly, Shakira's favorite color is periwinkle with glitter, and Lizzie likes shiny magenta.

"Hey, guys, guess what?" Sophia chimed in.

"What?" they replied together.

"Emma's going to be a famous TV news reporter!"

"Is that true?" Lizzie asked me.

"Sure is," I said. "I just have to find a good news story. I've been searching all day."

"Wow," Shakira said. "When you become famous, are you going to ride to school in a limo and wear a boa and a tiara?"

"No, she can't do that," claimed Lizzie. "That's what princesses do, not TV news reporters. TV reporters are rich. They have a million pairs of shoes and get to ride in a helicopter at work. Right, Emma?"

"Um . . . right," I said. "I'm going to do all of that." But I really had no idea what they were talking about. I knew TV reporters were special, and that's what I wanted most. To be special.

Sophia, Lizzie, Shakira, and I got up to join the lunch line. It was Pizza Day, and we got our slices of pizza and sat right back down as fast as we could. On Pizza Day, everyone makes sure to stay in their seats and eat. No dillydallying. That's the Pizza Day rule. If you get up and run around, then you can't eat pizza the following week on Pizza Day . . . and then you'll be the only kid without pizza for lunch that day. It happened to Shakira once, and she said it was not awesome.

Everyone from my class was eating pizza, except for Javier. I looked over at his table and noticed he was eating a hamburger with a special bun. That's because he's allergic to the whole wheat pizza crust.

Javier sits alone sometimes. Well, a lot of times. It might be because he likes to throw food in the air and try to catch it in his mouth. He makes weird robot noises when the food goes in his mouth. And even weirder noises when it misses and lands on the floor . . . or on someone's head. Geraldine the lunch lady is always benching him on Pizza Day, but he doesn't care. He can't eat the pizza, anyway.

The rest of us were busy eating our pizza when—

"Eww!"

Everyone started screaming. I looked up to see what had happened. I saw Javier standing with his hands on his head.

"Oh, gross!" he yelled. "Someone put a worm in my hamburger! Look, look—it's like a thousand centimeters long and swimming in the ketchup!"

All of us ran over to see. It was extra gross. The worm was brown and slimy and super wormy. The boys started laughing. The girls were screaming. They pretended like they were gonna throw up. Then the boys pretended they

were gonna throw up on the girls, and the girls started screaming even louder. Geraldine the lunch lady hurried over.

"What's going on here?" Geraldine said, hands on her hips. "Why is everyone breaking the Pizza Day rules? Do you all want meat loaf next week?"

"No, no . . . look," said Sophia. "Someone put a worm in Javier's hamburger!"

"It's a wormburger!" I said with disgust. Everyone started laughing again.

"Okay, enough. It's not funny, guys," said Geraldine in a serious voice. "Give me the wormburger—I mean, the hamburger—and let's get back to lunch."

Well, that was all anyone could talk about for the rest of lunch. Who would put a worm in Javier's hamburger?

"I can't believe Javier almost ate a worm," said Shakira.

"Eww!" offered Lizzie.

"I hope they figure out how it got there," said Sophia. "I don't want to find a worm in my food."

"Sophia!" I screamed with excitement. "That's brilliant!"

"Um—what's brilliant? The worm? That's gross!"

"I know it's gross," I said. "That's why it's brilliant. I can do a news story about Javier's wormburger! It's perfect. It's something true and that people want to know about. And it's not at all boring. Sophia, you're a genius!"

"Uh . . . you're welcome?" she replied.

"This is gonna be great! I'm gonna be sooo famous. Just wait, I'm gonna be the most famous kid that ever went to P.S. 387. Soon I'll be riding in a limo to school! I'll have to wear famous-style sunglasses. And famous-style jewelry and boas. Maybe I'll ride in a helicopter to school!"

Sophia rolled her eyes. But I hardly noticed. I felt famous already!

CHAPTER
FOUR

My First News Report

PAPI!" I screamed as soon as I heard him walk through the door of our apartment. "Papi, Papi, Papi . . . I found one! I found one!"

"You found one what?" he asked, putting his newspaper down.

"I found a news story! Well, I'm pretty sure I did."

"Give your father a minute to come inside," said Mom.

"Okay, come inside, Papi. But guess what?

There was a worm in Javier's hamburger at school today!"

"Huh," said Papi as he unzipped his coat and hung it up. "That sounds exciting . . . and disturbing. What happened?"

I followed Papi as he walked into the living room to pick up baby Mia, and told him all about Javier's wormburger.

Papi just smiled. And then he stared. He stared and smiled so much I started feeling weird.

"What?" I said.

"Did you hear that, Mia?" Papi asked my baby sister with that same smile.

"What?" I wanted to know.

"Your sister just told her first news story," Papi said as he nuzzled noses with Mia. She giggled.

"It's a good story, right, Papi?"

"Yup, you got a good one, kiddo. This is

something people need to know about. We want to make sure none of the other hamburgers at school have worms in them."

"Right!" I agreed.

"Breaking news from Emma Perez!" Papi said with a huge grin.

"I broke the news? It's broken?"

"No, silly, it's not broken. It means you'll be the first reporter to tell us about this news story."

"Wow."

My cat jumped into my arms. "What do you think, Luna?"

"Meow!" she replied.

I decided Luna could be my news reporter's assistant. Cats always make good assistants—especially for famous people.

Papi said we could work on my news story after dinner.

I waited until he ate his very last bite of spaghetti and sipped his very last sip of water. Just as he put his glass back on the table, I asked him, "Now, Papi? Can we do my news story now?"

"*Cálmate*, Emma. Relax. I'm still eating my dinner."

"No, you're not. You have no more spaghetti, your meatballs are all gone, and you drank your last sip of water."

"Can I have a minute to digest?"

"Okay, one minute," I allowed.

I started counting in my head. Once I counted sixty seconds, I tried again.

"Please, please, please, Papi!" I begged. "*¿Por favor?*"

"All right. You sound like a pushy reporter already."

"Why, thank you!" I beamed.

We went upstairs to my room, and Papi opened the laptop he gave me on my birthday. It used to be his, but I got to have it after he got a new one at work.

"Okay, let's see now," he said, adjusting the screen so the camera pointed at me.

"Ha-ha! It's me," I said as soon as I saw myself. Then I said, "Hellloooo, dahling. How aarrre you? This is Emma, and I'm on the air!"

"Sounding good in there," said Mom, stopping at the door with Mia in her arms.

"Actually, you're sounding great," said Papi. "Emma, that's a great name for your news show: 'Emma Is On the Air.'"

"'Emma Is On the Air!'" I repeated. "That sounds famous!"

"Yes, very famous," he said with a laugh.

"It's perfect," added Mom as she carried Mia off to take a bath.

"Okay," said Papi. "Do you really want to learn how to be a reporter?"

"Yes, please," I said. I could already tell this was going to be great.

"Remember when you told me about what happened to Javier's hamburger?"

"Yes."

"Well, now you're going to do the exact same thing, except we're going to record it on the computer."

"Got it!"

"Press the record button right there," instructed Papi, "and have at it."

I pressed record and looked right into the camera. I said, "This is Emma, and I'm on the air!" I looked over at Papi, and he was smiling.

"Keep going," he whispered.

Then I just started talking. I told the story about Javier's wormburger all over again. When I was done, we watched it back. It was so cool.

"Next we have to post your report to the school bulletin board," Papi explained. "That way people will be able to see 'Emma Is On the Air' on the Internet."

"And that way I'll be famous!" I shouted. I had to get up and start doing the famous jumpy dance. That's a dance you do when you know you're gonna be famous. This is how you do it: You spin around really fast and when you jump, you have to spread your legs wide-open, kinda like a ballerina but way more fun. And then you sing, *"I'm famous, I'm famous, I'm famous!"*

"Relax, *mija*. We all know you're famous," Papi said. I think he was starting to get irritated. Maybe he'd like it better if I sang in Spanish?

"¡Soy famosa! ¡Soy famosa! ¡Soy famosa!" I sang as I continued doing my dance.

"Emma," Papi said with a stern voice.

I took a deep breath and sat back down.

After we posted my very first "Emma Is On the Air" report, we watched it on the computer again. But after I watched it a second time, I realized that something was missing. I had a lot of questions. Like, how did the worm get into Javier's hamburger, anyway? Who put it there? And what happened afterward? Did he actually bite into it? Did he swallow the worm? Eww.

Did someone get in trouble? I told my papi about all the questions I still had.

"Those are all great questions, Emma," he said. "And you're right. Your story is not done yet. These are questions you should try to answer at school tomorrow."

"How do I do that?"

"By interviewing people. Find people who might have the answers to your questions, and then ask them what you want to know."

"But who has the answers?"

"You'll have to figure that part out. A good place to start is with witnesses. Find the people who saw what happened and ask them about it."

"Witnesses. Okay. The part I really want to know the most is, who did it? Who put the worm in Javier's hamburger?"

"The witnesses will help you figure that out," Papi said. "Each witness you interview will give you clues. Put all the clues together and you'll have your answer."

"Clues . . . That sounds like detective work."

"It is very similar to what a detective would do."

"Hey, detectives can be famous, too! So maybe I can be a reporter *and* a detective?" I asked.

"That sounds like a good plan to me," Papi said. "And it sounds like 'Emma Is On the Air' has work to do at school tomorrow."

"I think so, Papi. I think so."

CHAPTER
FIVE

Reporter-in-Training

PAPI drove me to school the next day so he could tell the principal about my news show and make sure it was okay for me to do my investigation.

"I bet Javier will be really grateful you took on his case, Emma," said Papi as he drove down the street.

"Yeah, especially since I heard his mom got really mad about it. Papi, would you get mad if I ate a worm in school?"

"Well, I wouldn't be thrilled," he said.

"What if it was just a nice worm who wanted to be friends with me and snuck into my hamburger because he knew I was so famous and he wanted to be famous, too? You can't get mad at that worm, right, Papi?"

"Uh-huh . . . okay. I guess not. We're here. You can undo your seat belt."

Papi and I walked into school and went straight to Principal Lee's office to get permission to investigate at school.

Principal Lee crossed her arms. "A reporter and a detective, huh?" she said.

"Yup," I said. "I only report on things that are true and things people need to know about. And we need to know how Javier's hamburger became a wormburger."

"Yes, I heard you posted something on the

online bulletin board last night," said Principal Lee. "A pretty good news report, from what I'm told."

I smiled. I knew I was famous!

"I gave her my old cell phone so she can use the camera to do interviews in school today," explained Papi. "The phone itself isn't hooked up. Is that all right?"

"I suppose so, as long as it doesn't interfere with your schoolwork, Emma," she said.

"Yippee! No, it won't. I promise!"

Now that I had permission, Papi said good-bye and left for work and I went to class.

"Okay, everyone have a seat," Miss Thompson said. "We'll be doing more with fractions today. Who can give an example of how we use fractions in our everyday lives?"

Miss Thompson is great, but I was pretty sure she wouldn't let me do my wormburger investigation in the middle of a fractions lesson. My investigation couldn't really begin until lunch, which wasn't until 12:15. I had to wait a long time to get there. Fractions, then sentences, then art projects representing our family heritages—school felt like it would take forever.

After I drew a picture and wrote about my favorite Dominican dish, it was finally time for lunch! In the cafeteria, I made sure I had everything I needed to start my investigation. My reporter/ detective tools were in my purple sparkle backpack:

Emma

I had the cell phone Papi gave me, plus a microphone he had.

Papi said you don't need a microphone when you do interviews on your phone, but I wanted to be just like the news reporter on TV. So we also added a cube with a big purple *E* for *Emma* to the top.

I had a shiny purple feather pencil with extra-special sparkles and a special purple reporter's pad to take notes.

All I needed now was to find someone to interview. Someone who might be able to answer my questions and give me some clues about how that worm got in Javier's hamburger. I spotted Javier sitting down to open his lunch. He was an important witness. He saw what happened because it happened to him! So I decided to talk to Javier first.

Sophia spotted me as I was walking toward Javier and called over, "Hey, Emma! Are you starting your wormburger investigation?"

"Yup! I'm about to do an interview with Javier. Hey, maybe you can help me?"

"Sure!" Sophia said excitedly.

"Can you hold my camera phone while I hold the microphone? Make sure you point it at Javier the whole time."

"Got it!"

We walked over to Javier's table and sat down across from him.

"Hey, Javier, we need to interview you." I put

my mic right in Javier's face. "You are a key witness in my wormburger investigation."

Javier smiled when he saw the camera and microphone. In fact, everyone started looking.

"Sure," Javier replied, sounding a little confused, but interested. "What's a wormburger investigation? Are you recording me?"

"Yup, yup, we're doing an interview for my news show," I said. "I'm a news reporter now, you know, and my first story is the Case of the Lunchroom Wormburger."

"Nice! Am I going to be on TV?" asked Javier.

"Yup," I said. "Well, you'll be on TV if you cooperate." Then all the kids started crowding behind him because they wanted to be on TV, too.

That started making me feel a little nervous. Everyone was staring. To be honest, I'm not really used to being stared at. Kids at school don't usually pay much attention to me—especially boys. What if they laughed at my news show? I thought for a minute that this might not be such a good idea. I looked at Sophia, unsure what to do.

"Come on, Emma," Sophia whispered. "Just ignore them. You can do it."

I took a deep breath and continued.

"Now, Javier," I said in my best reporter voice, "I need to know exactly what happened yesterday when you found a worm in your hamburger."

"Oh, yeah." Javier laughed. "That was pretty nasty." The kids around us started laughing. Sophia smiled, encouraging me to continue.

"Yes," I said. I glared at the other kids, trying to hold the microphone away from them so it wouldn't just be filled with the noise of their laughter. "But, Javier, what happened? And it has to be the truth."

"Right, right . . . well, let me see . . . yesterday I had a worm in my hamburger," he explained.

I rolled my eyes. "Yes, Javier, I know that part already. But how did it get there?"

"Hmm. I don't know," he said.

Why couldn't Javier just *focus*? Some people . . .

But then he continued, "Oh, yeah, it was Pizza Day. But I'm allergic to whole wheat, so my mom gave me a leftover hamburger with a gluten-free bun. My mom told Miss Thompson to ask the cook to heat it up for me at lunch."

"Uh-huh," I said.

Then Javier's friend Adrian shouted from the crowd, "Your mom made you a worm-burger?"

"No!" Javier yelled back. He looked embarrassed, and I felt bad for him.

I gave Adrian the reporter's look of death

and said, "Adrian. This is a serious investigation. Either watch in silence or keep it moving!"

"Ooohh," hissed the other kids.

Finally, everyone was quiet, and I said, "Okay, Javier, continue."

"So at lunch, Miss Thompson gave my hamburger to Geraldine the lunch lady, so she could give it to Beatrice the cook. Then I got in the lunch line with my tray just like everyone else. By the time I got inside the kitchen, Beatrice had my hamburger . . . I mean, my wormburger," Javier said with a laugh, "ready for me. So I took my plate with the wormburger. I grabbed a milk and a salad and sat down at the table."

"Wait a minute," I said. "The worm came from your house?"

"No!" said Javier. "I only noticed the worm as I was taking my second bite."

"So you took one bite and there was no worm. Then you took a second bite and saw a squiggly worm staring at you?" I asked.

"Yeah. That's what happened," replied Javier.

"And you're sure there was no worm in that burger before you got to school?" I asked.

"Nope, definitely not. I saw my mom get the hamburger ready. No worms at all," Javier insisted.

"Hmm. Okay, thanks, Javier," I said.

"Wait, wait," he said.

"Yes?"

"Well, I was thinking . . . what if Geraldine the lunch lady was possessed by a worm-loving mutant hawk? And the hawk flew down and took over her body and she went out to the playground and got a worm and put it in my hamburger because she thought a wormburger would taste awesome. Think that's what happened?" Javier asked—in a serious voice.

"Um. Yeah, okay," I replied. "I guess that's possible. But I still have some more witnesses to interview. So . . . yeah. We'll see."

Javier started to pretend he was Geraldine the lunch lady possessed by a mutant hawk. He was pretending to fly around the table with his hands in the air, taking swipes at his lunch with just his mouth. The kids around us giggled and went back to eating lunch. I walked away, too.

I didn't have time to talk about Javier's wild theories; he didn't notice, but Javier had just given me my first clue! I was about to break this story wide open!

CHAPTER SIX

My First Clues

SOPHIA and I sat down at the next table to talk about the clue we found.

"Wow, Emma," Sophia said. "A lot of people touched Javier's hamburger."

"You're right," I said. "I need to keep track of them all."

I pulled out my purple reporter's pad and my shiny purple feather pencil.

I wrote Emma's Official Reporter's Pad at the top. On the first page, I wrote, News

Report #1: The Case of the Lunchroom Wormburger. And then wrote underneath that:

Clue #1: The hamburger became a wormburger after Javier gave it to Miss Thompson, who gave it to Geraldine the lunch lady, who gave it to Beatrice the cook.

"So the worm wasn't in the hamburger before Javier gave it to Miss Thompson?" asked Sophia.

"Nope."

"Then when did the worm get inside there? Do you think Miss Thompson did it, Emma?" Sophia wondered aloud.

"Not a chance. She would never," I insisted. I couldn't help but wonder if she did, though. I really liked Miss Thompson and didn't want to believe she was guilty. But I figured a good reporter couldn't let her personal feelings get in the way of an investigation. I spotted Miss Thompson across the lunchroom.

"Sophia, we better go interview Miss Thompson to be sure."

Sophia and I ran across the lunchroom, and I called in my super-famous voice, "MISS THOMPSON!"

She turned around.

"Whoa, Emma. Not so loud, please. Why aren't you girls eating your lunches?" she asked.

"Miss Thompson, there's no time to eat today," I said, panting a little.

"Yeah, no time at all!" Sophia added.

"We're in the middle of a wormburger investigation, and you are the next witness!" I explained.

"I'm sorry, you're in the middle of what?" Miss Thompson looked confused.

"We're trying to figure out who put the worm in Javier's hamburger yesterday," I told her.

"Ah," she said.

"Miss Thompson, you may not have heard yet, but I am very famous," I said. "I solve mysteries and report them on my news show. This is my first case. I've got to get to the bottom of this wormburger situation," I explained in my very official reporter–sounding voice. That's a voice that's serious. That way people take you seriously.

"Sounds exciting. What can I do for you?" she asked.

I held up the microphone. "I'm interviewing all the witnesses and putting them in my news show." I signaled to Sophia to press record.

"Javier told us that when he brought the hamburger to school, it didn't have a worm in it. But then he gave it to you to give to Geraldine to give to Beatrice to heat up at lunchtime. Before you had it, no worm. After you had it, worm."

"Uh-huh," was all Miss Thompson said. I started getting nervous about what I was going to ask her next.

"So . . . I was wondering . . ." I stammered.

"Yes, Emma?"

"Well, Miss Thompson, I was wondering . . . did *you* put the worm in Javier's hamburger?" I asked the last part really fast. I thought maybe if I said it quickly she wouldn't get mad. But then Miss Thompson started laughing. She didn't look mad at all.

"I guess that's a fair question," she said.

"Right, thanks, Miss Thompson. But . . . did you put the worm in Javier's hamburger?"

"No. I didn't," she replied. "I was shocked to find out that there was a worm in there. Javier's parents were pretty upset and Principal Lee had to get involved. I had to skip my plans to plant tomatoes in our organic garden behind the school yard."

"I see," I said, nodding in an official-reporter way. "Can you tell us exactly what you did with the hamburger after Javier gave it to you?"

"Sure," she said. "I gave it to Geraldine and explained that, according to Javier's mom, it just needed to be warmed up for a few minutes. Then he could get it from the kitchen with all the other kids waiting in the hot lunch line. I can't be certain the worm wasn't in there yet, but the burger looked fine to me."

"Okay. Just like that, you gave it to Geraldine? No one else touched it?" I asked.

"Not that I saw," Miss Thompson said. "And I'm sure Geraldine wouldn't put a worm in someone's hamburger. She's been our lunch lady for seventeen years. I can't imagine she would ever do anything like that."

"Hmm," I said.

"Emma, the health inspector heard about what happened and is going to visit the school to investigate. She could decide that someone should be fired for this. So if you get to the bottom of the mystery, let us know!"

"Okay, Miss Thompson. I'm on the case! And since I'm famous that means everything will be okay. You don't have to worry."

"Thank you, Emma," Miss Thompson said.

Now I knew this case was important, just like Papi said a news story should be.

"Sophia, I have to solve this case before the health inspector arrives. I don't want Miss Thompson to get in trouble."

"Yeah, she said she didn't do it, and I believe her," said Sophia.

I pulled out my official reporter's pad and my shiny purple feather pencil and wrote down:

Clue #2: Miss Thompson gave the
   hamburger to Geraldine. No worm
   yet. Health inspector investigating.

Then Geraldine the lunch lady started telling the kids that lunchtime was over.

"Time's up. Let's go, out the door."

I hadn't eaten a single bite of my sandwich, but I wasn't hungry, anyway. This case was getting good. I packed up my tools and started to get in line with Sophia and everyone else when I noticed Geraldine cleaning up in the kitchen.

I started picturing her as a possessed mutant hawk who plucked a worm from the playground, like Javier had said. And then I noticed something peculiar. Inside the kitchen on top of a cabinet were a watering can, a pair of gardening gloves, and a shovel. *That's odd,* I thought. *Why would garden tools be in the kitchen?*

I popped out of line and snuck into the kitchen to get a closer look. Maybe there were worms inside. While no one was paying attention, I looked at the gardening things. I peeked inside the watering can and picked up the gloves

and the shovel to see if
I could feel any worms.
But all I felt was dirt. Eww. *Muy asqueroso.* So
gross. It looked like dried soil was caked on
everything. I wasn't sure what it meant, but I
decided this could be a clue. So I pulled out my
phone and shot some video of the gardening
tools. Then I wrote in my reporter pad:

Clue #3: Dirty gardening tools on
the kitchen cabinet. No worms.

I remembered Miss Thompson said that she
was supposed to work in the organic garden.
Were those her gardening tools? If those were
her gardening tools, what were they doing in
the school kitchen? Was there a chance she *did*
put the worm in Javier's hamburger?

CHAPTER
SEVEN

"Emma Is On the Air"

WHEN I got home from school, I told Luna everything that had happened and showed her all my clues. After dinner, Papi helped me transfer all my interviews onto the computer. Luna jumped up on my lap and snuggled in for our next reporter lesson.

"Now that you've started an investigation, you're working more like a real reporter," Papi told me after all the interviews popped up on the computer screen. "So this time you have to write your story into a script. And when you do your news update, you'll read the script."

Ugh. Writing.

"But, Papi, writing is hard. Famous people don't have to write!" I declared. "Don't you agree, Luna?"

"Meow!"

"Exactly."

"Emma, I know quite a few real TV news reporters, and they write all their own scripts," said Papi.

"Oh, great," I said with a sigh. Being famous was starting to seem really hard.

"Come on. No sulking. You can write your own script. We'll start off doing it together," said Papi. "What's the worst that can happen?"

"The worst that can happen?" I cried. "What if the script I write is terrible? What if everyone hates it?"

"Well, that would be great!" Papi said with a smile. My papi really is weird.

"Weird, Papi," I said.

"What I mean is who cares if it's terrible? At least you did it. And then you can do it again next time, and it can be a little less terrible. And then you can keep trying and trying and eventually, you know what, I bet it won't be terrible at all." Now Papi was getting excited.

"So you want me to write a terrible script?" I asked. That sounded silly.

"Yes! Let's see how terrible we can make it!"

Luna pawed at my face like she was trying

to make me laugh, too. I started giggling, just a little. "Okay," I said. "One terrible script coming right up." So I took out my shiny purple feather pencil and my reporter's pad and started writing. Luna jumped onto the desk next to me.

"Remember," Papi said, "you want to tell everyone what happened today during your investigation, and then you can pause in the middle to play parts of your interviews so they can hear what the witnesses said."

"Right," I said.

I had to write the first sentence four times because I kept messing up. I didn't really want to write the most terrible script ever. But once I got the first sentence right, the rest came out really easily. This is what I wrote:

News Update:

This is Emma, and I'm on the air!

My first sentence sounded amazing—and famous! Then I wrote:

Here's an update on the wormburger
investigation. Today at lunchtime,
I found three new clues. #1: Javier
brought in the hamburger from home
because he's allergic to whole-wheat
pizza. He gave it to Miss Thompson,
who gave it to Geraldine the lunch
lady, who gave it to Beatrice the
cook to heat up. Now listen to my
interview with Javier.

Then I left a space where I planned to press
play on Javier's interview.

#2: Miss Thompson says she gave the
hamburger to Geraldine and there
was no worm inside. The principal
and the health inspector are doing

their own investigation. Now listen
to my interview with Miss Thompson.

Then I left a space where I planned to play
my interview with Miss Thompson. Then I wrote:

#3: I found dirty gardening tools in
the school kitchen. Take a look
at them. They were caked with
mud, but they didn't have any worms
on them. I'm not sure what that
means yet. I'm going to hold on to
this clue and see if I can make
sense of it later.

Dad looked at my script and said with a big
smile, "*Princesa*, this is the best—I mean, the
most *terrible*—script I've ever read. Nice work!"

I started laughing. I felt proud but also a little embarrassed. Then Papi said, "Now, why don't you write something in your script that says good-bye to all your viewers."

So then I wrote at the end:

That's all I learned today. But the wormburger investigation continues tomorrow! I'll see you then.

"Perfect. ¡Perfecto!" Papi said.

CHAPTER EIGHT

Professional Pretty

AFTER I finished writing my script, Papi stayed with me while I set up the computer to start recording.

"I look goooood!" I said.

"Muy bonita," said Papi.

"But wait. I think I could look better . . ."

I jumped out of my desk chair, ran out of my room and into my parents' bedroom, and headed straight for my mom's closet. Luna ran right after me.

"MOM?" I called. She was downstairs on the phone.

"What, hon?" she yelled back.

"Can I borrow your green velvet blazer with the patches on the elbows, please?"

"Sure."

"Where is it?" I yelled again. But she didn't answer. "MOM," I called one more time. "I can't fiiind it!" And then I turned around and jumped. My mom was right behind me.

"No more yelling, Em," she said.

"Sorry," I said. "I can't find the blazer."

"Hmm." Mom looked around in the back of the closet and started tugging at something. She pulled and pulled and pulled. Then I grabbed it, too, and we both started pulling and pulling and pulling . . . until it finally came out and we both fell on the floor.

"Oops." I laughed.

"Let's see if it fits," said Mom. "Is this for your news show?"

"Yup, yup." I put the jacket on over my purple T-shirt. "What do you think? Do I look famous?"

"Yes, I would say so. You look very famous."

I spotted her old pearl necklace.

Mom saw me staring at it and said, "Here. Take this, too."

The pearls felt cold as Mom put them around my neck.

"There. You look great," she said with a smile. "Have fun."

"Thanks, Mom!"

I ran back to my room. Reporters need to run a lot. That's what they do. I don't know why, but on TV, they're always in a hurry. So I was like a lightning bolt, right back into my desk chair—this time wearing the green velvet blazer and white pearl necklace.

"What do you think? Famous?" I asked Papi and Luna.

Luna meowed in approval, and Papi said *"Sí."*

Now I was ready. I fixed my chocolate pudding-Slinky curls so they were just right. Then I tilted the camera so it was pointed at me. And I couldn't believe how I looked. I didn't have any lip gloss or blush, but I felt just like the fancy reporter from TV. I looked professional, and I couldn't help it when my lips curled into a super smile.

I grabbed my Emma microphone and called Luna to come sit on my lap. She was a reporter, too, after all. She had to help. I clicked the red record button. Then I looked down at my script and spoke into the microphone.

"This is Emma, and I'm on the air!" And then I stopped. I wanted to try again with a louder, more reporter-y voice. I cleared my throat and said, "This is Emma, and I'm on the air!" And I sang the last part! It was so funny, Papi started laughing.

Then I read my script out loud. After I read each paragraph, I paused to play the interview that matched. When I was done with all three clues, I hit the record button again to stop. We were finished.

Papi and I watched it again all put together. It. Was. Awesome.

"You did a great job with your investigation today, *mija*. I'm proud of you," Papi said as he posted it on my school's website. He had that weird grin again.

"Thanks, Papi," I said. "But there's so much more to do. You heard Miss Thompson. The health inspector is coming, and someone might get fired! I have to solve the case before anything bad happens."

"Okay, then we'd better go to bed and get some rest. You've got lots of investigating to do!"

"Okay."

"Buenas noches, mija," Papi said as he kissed my forehead. "Good night."

CHAPTER
NINE

Back to School

LUNA, what are you doing on the counter?"
I heard my dad saying the next morning. "You
know you're not supposed to be there."

"She's making my coffee, Papi," I explained as I came into the kitchen. *Duh.*

"Ah, well then. Carry on," said Papi.

All reporters drink coffee. That's a fact. Papi drinks it every morning. I don't like coffee, so Luna and I had chocolate milk with foam in a coffee cup. Then we went back upstairs to get dressed.

"Luna," I said, "I'm gonna wear my green reporter blazer to school today. It looks more professional to do an investigation with a green velvet blazer." Luna agreed. So I put on my blazer, a purple shimmer T-shirt, and a pair of jeans—plus the pearls. Then I made sure I packed my cell phone camera, my microphone, my reporter's pad, and my shiny purple feather pencil in my backpack.

I tried as hard as I could to listen in class, but secretly I couldn't wait for lunch. In the early morning, we had music and reading time, which were great. But then after reading time, we had a poetry lesson, and that was not great.

"Who wants to read their poem to the class?" Miss Thompson asked.

I definitely did not, so I did not raise my hand.

"Ooh, I do, I do."

That was Melissa G. Of course Melissa G. wanted to read her poem. She always volunteers to be in front of the class. She thinks everyone wants to watch her because she was on TV before, in *one* toothpaste commercial. She didn't even say anything. All she did was brush her teeth and smile. But she told everyone all about it, and everyone said she was so famous.

Humph.

"Miss Thompson, my poem is about how important it is to brush your teeth."

"That sounds interesting. Go ahead, Melissa."

Melissa began to read her poem, but I couldn't even listen. What kind of poem is that? She just wanted to remind people how famous she was. Finally Melissa G. was almost done.

"So if you brush every day, all your cavities will go away. Your smile will be bright as the sun, and you can be the famous one!"

"Thank you, Melissa. Very nice. Have a seat. Who else wants a turn?"

That was silly. Brushing your teeth to be famous? I was going to solve a mystery and save

Miss Thompson from the health inspector! I started thinking maybe that was even better than being famous. Hmm.

After three more poems, Miss Thompson told us it was time for lunch. As we were walking to the lunchroom, I spotted a woman I'd never seen before. She was tall and wore her light blond hair in a really tight bun on the back of her head. She had glasses, held a clipboard, and was walking with Principal Lee. She didn't look very nice.

When we all got to the lunchroom, I asked Miss Thompson, "Who was that lady with Principal Lee?"

"That was the health inspector," Miss Thompson replied in a whisper. She looked nervous.

"Oh, no," I said as I put my hand to my mouth.

"Don't worry about it, Emma. It'll be just fine. Go eat your lunch."

But I *was* worried about it. I knew that time was running out, and I had to solve the case of the lunchroom wormburger today—or someone would get in trouble.

CHAPTER
TEN

The Hunt for a Wormer

THE next witness on my list was Geraldine the lunch lady. I got my camera and my microphone ready and headed straight for the front of the lunch line, where Geraldine was standing, making sure kids didn't cut. I didn't run like a reporter, because you aren't allowed to run in the cafeteria. But I walked really fast—until I had to stop because Sophia, Lizzie, and Shakira were calling out to me.

"Emma, Emma," they said, hurrying over.

"Hey, guys," I said.

"We saw your report last night. Are you working on your investigation right now?" asked Lizzie.

"Yup, yup, I sure am," I said proudly.

"So do you know who turned Javier's hamburger into a wormburger yet?" asked Shakira.

"Not yet," answered Sophia. "Right, Emma? You need more clues and more interviews."

"Exactly. I'm about to interview my next witness, Geraldine the lunch lady. Wanna come, Sophia?"

"Can't," Sophia replied. "My mom says I have to eat my lunch today."

"Oh, okay. I think I can manage. See you guys later!"

I spotted Geraldine near the kitchen and walked over to her.

"Geraldine?" I said a little timidly.

"Yes," she said with a huff. She looked very busy.

"Can I talk to you for a second?"

"Make it quick. It's Taco Day, and everybody's taking too long picking their toppings." She pointed to my reporter supplies. "Hey, what's that thing?"

"It's my camera. I need to interview you for my news show. It's called 'Emma Is On the Air,' and you are my next witness," I explained.

"Witness? What did I witness?"

"You were there when Javier found a worm in his hamburger the other day."

"Oh, yes, you're right," she said. She didn't seem to mind that I was recording, so I kept going.

"Miss Thompson said she gave the hamburger to you before there was a worm inside," I explained.

"Right. Miss Thompson asked me to hand it over to Beatrice to heat it up for Javier. So I did," she said.

"That's it? You just gave it to Beatrice the cook? Did you look at the hamburger?" I asked.

"Well, now that you mention it, Javier's mom wrapped it in aluminum foil. And you can't put aluminum foil in a microwave. So I grabbed a cardboard container and put the hamburger inside. *Then* I gave it to Beatrice. And I didn't see a worm in there."

"Interesting," I said. "Very interesting." I was pretty sure I'd found my next clue. "Thanks, Geraldine!" I said as I ran off.

"You're welcome, Emma," called Geraldine after me. "Emma—no running! Hey, Dave, cheese, tomatoes, lettuce, and salsa ... pick a topping and move on. There are other kids who need to eat ..."

I run-walk-shuffled to a table, pulling out my purple reporter's pad and my shiny purple feather pencil. I hurriedly wrote:

Clue #4. Geraldine took the hamburger out of the aluminum foil and put it into a microwavable cardboard box before she gave it to Beatrice. No worm.

Hmm. A cardboard box. I thought about that for a minute. I was starting to get a pretty good idea of how that worm might have gotten into Javier's hamburger, but I needed to do a few more interviews. I ran over to Miss Thompson and asked her a question, without the camera this time.

"Miss Thompson . . . you said you were supposed to work on the organic garden by the school yard two days ago, right?"

"Yes, that's right. I never got a chance to, though," she replied.

"I know. But do you know who was working on it *before* lunch?"

"Yes, it was Mr. Delmonico. He picked a group of kids to work on a special school project, planting zucchini for the bake sale next semester. For zucchini bread."

"Javier's in that group, right?" I asked.

"I believe so."

Lizzie and Shakira are in that same group. I had to find them. Fast.

"Thanks, Miss Thompson!"

"You're welcome—and, Emma, stop running!"

CHAPTER ELEVEN

A Pretty Good Idea
What Happened

I **HURRIED** over to my regular lunch table. Sophia was eating tacos with Lizzie and Shakira—exactly the people I needed to talk to.

"Hi, guys. Wanna be famous? Wanna be on my show?" I asked in a hurry.

"Sure!" they said together with mouths full of taco meat and cheese. We all started laughing.

"Sorry, Emma," they said, still giggling. As soon as they were done swallowing, I set up my cell phone camera.

"Can I hold the camera again?" offered Sophia.

"That would be great!" I gave it to Sophia, and she pressed record.

"So," I said. "Lizzie and Shakira, were you guys planting zucchini in the organic garden by the school yard the day before yesterday?" I asked.

Shakira answered first. "Yes! It was so much fun!"

"No," said Lizzie.

"No, you weren't planting zucchini?" I asked, a little confused.

"Yes, we were planting zucchini, but I mean no, it wasn't fun. It was so gross. We had to get dirty and mucky. It was not fun, Shakira," Lizzie said.

"Yes, it was. I had a blast," Shakira insisted.

I needed to interrupt. "Can you guys answer a question for me? Did you see Javier there? In the garden?" I asked.

"Oh, yeah, Javier was there," Lizzie said. "He was really into it. He even asked Mr. Delmonico if he could take some of the soil and seeds home with him to plant his own zucchini garden."

"He did?" I asked. "Did Mr. Delmonico let him?"

"No, Mr. Delmonico said no," explained Shakira. "He said if Javier's parents wanted to let him plant a zucchini garden at home, then they would have to tell Mr. Delmonico, who would help them find the seeds. He said Javier couldn't just take everything home without asking his parents first. Javier looked upset. He was so upset he asked to go to the bathroom before we were finished."

"Yeah," continued Lizzie, "he didn't even come back outside. We met up with him after we finished in the garden and saw him walking through the lunchroom."

Yes! I knew it! I pulled out my reporter's pad and wrote:

Clue #5: Javier planted zucchini in
   the garden and left early to go
   to the bathroom.

"Did we help?" Lizzie asked.
"Are we gonna be on TV?" asked Shakira.

"Yes! You guys were awesome! I gotta go. Thanks for your help!"

I had one more interview to do, and I was pretty sure the mystery would be solved. Sophia handed me the camera, and I ran over to Beatrice in the kitchen.

"*Hola*, Beatrice," I said. Beatrice speaks Spanish, too.

"*Hola, linda,*" she said back. "*¿Cómo estás?*" That means "Hello, beautiful. How are you?" You say it like this: OH-la, LEEN-da. KO-mo es-TAHS?

"I'm okay," I said in English. I had to hurry. I had a feeling the health inspector would be here soon.

"Beatrice, remember when you heated up Javier's hamburger on Monday?"

"Ah, let's see. Yes, yes, I remember."

"Well, when you saw it, did it have a worm inside?" I asked.

"Ay, claro que no, mi amor," she said. That means "Oh, of course not, my love."

"That's what I thought," I said. "One more question. Did you see Javier in the kitchen before lunch?"

"Oh, yes. He came here from the garden with one of those watering cans full of dirt! He asked me for a cardboard container. I gave him one and then he put all the dirt from the watering can into it. *Que asqueroso,"* she said, wrinkling her nose. "Who knows what was in there! I told him to get out of the kitchen with that stuff. He ran off, and he forgot to take his gardening tools back outside. He left them over there." She pointed to the countertop. "They were in the way, so I moved them to the cabinet. I completely forgot they're still there! Thanks for reminding me. I'm gonna figure out where they need to go after lunch."

"Thanks, Beatrice!" I started running out of the kitchen. *"¡Gracias!"*

"Okay, *mi amor. Adios.* See you later. Don't run!"

As soon as I found a place to sit, I pulled out my reporter's pad and wrote:

Clue #6: Beatrice the cook saw Javier pour soil from a watering can into a cardboard container.

That was all I needed to know. I was almost positive the case was solved. I just needed to ask Javier a few more questions . . .

"Okay, kids, line up. Lunch is over," called Geraldine. "It's too rainy for yard time, so Miss Thompson's class, go to the computer lab. Mr. Smith's class is going to the library. Miss Shaw's class . . ."

Oh, no! I thought. *I'm out of time!*

I had to talk to Javier and write my report so that everyone would know what really happened. And I had to do it fast, because just behind Miss Thompson, I saw Principal Lee walking into the lunchroom—with the health inspector!

Uh-oh.

CHAPTER
TWELVE

Mystery Solved

TIME was ticking, and I didn't know what to do. I started scanning the lunchroom for ideas—

Then I saw it. A lunch box, a sweater, and two hats on the floor.

"Miss Thompson!" I shouted with my hand raised high.

"What is it, Emma?"

"Javier left his sweater on the floor. I also see a lunch box and two hats. Can we go pick them up?"

"Sure, but hurry."

I ran over to Javier in line and pulled his arm.

"Whoa ... okay, I'm coming," he said as I dragged him toward the other side of the lunchroom.

"You forgot your sweater, Javier," I said, loud enough for the class to hear. Then I pulled him behind a closet door and pressed record.

"We only have a minute, Javier, but I have to ask you a few more questions."

"What?"

"The day you found the worm in your hamburger, you also took soil from the organic garden so you could grow your own zucchini at home, right?"

Javier started looking around like he was checking to see if anyone else could hear.

"Uh, I don't know, Emma," he answered sheepishly.

"I think you do know," I replied. And then I explained the whole thing. I told Javier what I thought really happened. I told him why I thought *he* was the one who put the worm in his own hamburger.

"I . . . um . . . I . . ." he said. Then finally, he said, "Ugh. I guess you might be right. It's probably my fault. But, Emma, I swear I didn't do it on purpose."

"I know you didn't," I said, trying to comfort him. "Don't worry about it. It's not a big deal right now, but it will be if I don't write my report before the health inspector finds someone else to blame."

Javier and I raced back to our class. When we got to the computer lab, I sat down and took a deep breath. Now I knew for sure that Miss Thompson did *not* put that worm in Javier's hamburger. And neither did Geraldine the lunch lady or Beatrice the cook.

I pulled out my reporter's pad. This was the worst part—writing. But there was nó time to be nervous. People needed to know the truth, and they needed to know it fast. So I started writing. And then I wrote some more. And then I realized, it was easier this time. I knew exactly what I wanted to say. It felt like my shiny purple feather pencil was taking over. Before I knew it, I was done.

Luckily the computer in the lab was a lot like our computer at home. So I got it ready just like my dad showed me. I sat up straight and looked into the camera. I saw myself on the computer screen, just like before. I was already wearing my green velvet blazer and my pearls, which made me giggle. This was so cool.

I cleared my throat, held my Emma microphone with confidence, and started reading.

"Hello, everyone. This is Emma, and I'm on the air! I've finally solved the case of the lunchroom wormburger. If the principal and health inspector are watching, please stop what you're doing and watch the rest of my report before you look for someone to blame.

"Yesterday I told you about how I discovered that Miss Thompson gave the hamburger to Geraldine, who gave it to Beatrice. And I also told you about the dirty gardening tools I found in the kitchen. Today I know what it all means. And today I can tell you that Javier put the worm in his own hamburger. But it was an accident. He didn't even know he did it. Let me explain."

I talked about everything I had learned at lunch. The aluminum foil, the cardboard burger box, the zucchini planting, and finally, how Javier put gardening soil in a cardboard box that looked just like the one Geraldine used for Javier's hamburger. I played all the witness interviews so people could hear it for themselves.

"Then I knew what really happened," I read. "I knew how Javier's hamburger became a wormburger. So I ran to find Javier and interviewed him a second time. Take a listen."

Then I pressed play on my most recent interview with Javier.

CHAPTER
THIRTEEN

The Final Interview

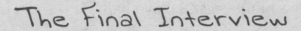

Emma: The day you found the worm
in your hamburger, you also took
soil from the organic garden so you
could grow your own zucchini at
home, right?

Javier: Uh, I don't know, Emma.

Emma: I think you do know.

Javier: Okay, okay. Yeah, I took some
soil from the garden. I just wanted
to make my own zucchini garden

at home. What's wrong with that?
I like zucchini bread!

Emma: I'm sure Mr. Delmonico would
be upset, but I don't care about
that part. Javier, think about
it. You put soil into a cardboard
container that looked just like
the container Beatrice used to
heat up your hamburger.

Javier: So . . .

Emma: So that's how your hamburger
became a wormburger.

Javier: What do you mean?

Emma: You had both cardboard boxes on
your table at lunch, right?

Javier: Yeah, I guess so.

Emma: You said you took one bite of
your hamburger and then put it

down. When you picked it up to take
a second bite, you saw the worm.

Javier: Yeah . . .

Emma: Javier, when you put your
hamburger down after the first
bite, you must have put it down in
the wrong box. You put it in the
box with the soil—a box of soil that
probably had worms inside. One of
them smelled your hamburger and
decided to crawl right in. When
you picked the hamburger back up
for your second bite, the worm had
already made a nice little home
for himself inside. <u>Bam!</u> Your
hamburger was a wormburger!

Javier: I thought I kept those boxes
separate . . . but Adrian wanted to

see the soil, so I opened the soil
box. I must have forgotten to
close it.

Emma: Thought so.

Javier: I . . . um . . . I . . . Ugh. I guess
you might be right. It's probably my
fault. But, Emma, I swear I didn't
do it on purpose.

Emma: I know you didn't.

I pressed stop on the interview and wrapped up my report.

"So, there you have it. How did a worm get inside Javier's hamburger? It crawled inside from Javier's soil box. It was just an accident. The case of the lunchroom wormburger is officially solved.

"Ms. Health Inspector, I hope you're watching. No one needs to get fired. It was all an accident.

"Thanks, everyone, for watching this edition of 'Emma Is On the Air.' I'll see you next time!"

Then I had to post my report on the school bulletin board. I remembered all the buttons Papi clicked—and presto! Done. I ran over to Miss Thompson and told her to watch it right away.

CHAPTER
FOURTEEN

Case Closed

P**URRR,**" Luna said as she sat in my lap at home that night.

"Aw, thanks, Luna. I know you wanted to be there. I was thinking about you the whole time."

"Meeeoow," Luna said with a happy purr. She was really proud of me. I could tell.

There was a knock on my bedroom door.

"Come in," I said as I sat on my bed feeling satisfied—and, of course, famous!

"Hi, *mija*," said Papi, leaning through the

doorway. "I heard about what happened at school today. Principal Lee called."

Principal Lee had spoken to me at school, too. She showed my report to the health inspector, and they both went to talk to Javier and learned the truth. Principal Lee was glad none of her staff members got in trouble. And she thanked me.

Everyone else at school saw my report, too. It was awesome. People were patting me on the back and saying I looked so cool. That was neat because people don't usually think I am cool. Sometimes it feels like they don't even know I'm there. Well, not anymore! Now I am *famous*! I sang the word in my head. And laughed. I was so busy thinking about school I forgot my papi was there.

"Hello? Emma? Are you gonna answer my question?"

"Oh, sorry, Papi. What was that?"

"I was saying, you did a great job this week. Not only did you solve the mystery and write a report all by yourself, but you know what else you did?"

"What?" I asked.

"You helped people. You helped Principal Lee protect Miss Thompson and Geraldine and Beatrice. And you helped Javier figure out the mistake he made. And now we all know that the kitchen at school is clean and safe. Thanks to you. Nice work."

I smiled as Papi left my room. Wow. He was right. I did help people. I started thinking again that maybe the helping part felt better than the famous part.

Nah—that is silly. Being famous is the best! I started doing the famous jumpy dance with Luna.

"*We're famous! We're famous! We're famous!*"
I sang.

Luna took off running around the room,
and I chased her. And then I fell on the floor,
laughing.

"I'm counting on you, kitty . . . my little *gatita*.
We're going to solve every mystery on the
planet! We'll be"—I stopped to sing—"*famous!
¡Somos famosas!* Come on, Luna, we have to go
find our next case!"

EMMA'S TIPS FOR NOT-BORING NEWS

1. Find a news story that's super awesome. I like stories about bugs that crawl into food. But you should pick a story that <u>you</u> like— that way, you won't have to go to the hospital for boredom overload!

2. Wear news clothes that are awesome. I always wear my green velvet blazer and my pearl necklace, but you can wear more than one necklace, or instead of a

blazer, a raincoat. Even if it's not raining. Ha-ha!

3. **Sing the news!** It's super funny when you sing your news report. Sometimes I sing, "This is Emma . . . and I'm on the aaaiiirrrrr." Luna always cracks up.

4. **Do the famous jumpy dance!** The famous jumpy dance is a good way to be famous. Your cat or dog can do it, too. Even your brother or sister, but <u>only</u> if they are not mean and promise not to touch your stuff.

See? Totally boring-proof!

Emma will be back ON THE AIR in

#2: PARTY DRAMA!